One morning when Sarah woke up, her rotten cat

Ralph was searching through the closet.

"I hope she got me what I wanted for my birthday,"

Ralph thought to himself.

"Happy birthday," said Sarah.

She gave him a hug and closed the closet door.

"Now, no snooping until your party."

Rotten Ralph made an ugly face and squirted toothpaste into Sarah's slippers.

"You are truly rotten, Ralph," she said.

# HAPPY BIRTHDAY ROTTEN RALPH

Written by Jack Gantos and Illustrated by Nicole Rubel

Houghton Mifflin Company
Boston

Happy 2nd Birthday Elliot!!
Your Pal,
Ryder
xoxo

**For Anne — J.G.**
**To my family — N.R.**

*Library of Congress Cataloging-in-Publication Data*

Gantos, Jack.
  Happy birthday Rotten Ralph/written by Jack Gantos; illustrated by Nicole Rubel.
  p. cm.
  Summary: Rotten Ralph the cat is up to his usual rotten behavior as Sarah prepares for his birthday party.
  RNF ISBN 0-395-53766-5    PAP ISBN 0-395-70091-4
  [1. Cats - Fiction.  2. Behavior - Fiction.  3. Birthdays - Fiction.  4. Parties - Fiction.]  I. Rubel, Nicole, ill.  II. Title.
PZ7.G15334Hap   1990                90-32738
[E] — dc20                          CIP
                                    AC

The character of Rotten Ralph was originally created by
Jack Gantos and Nicole Rubel.

Text copyright © 1990 by John B. Gantos, Jr.
Illustrations copyright © 1990 by Leslie Nicole Rubel

Printed in China

SCP   20 19 18 17 16 15 14 13 12

"We have to make a list of friends to invite,"
said Sarah.

Rotten Ralph wanted to invite all his alley-
cat friends. But Sarah wanted to invite his
sweet house-cat friends.

So Rotten Ralph poured prune juice onto her cereal.

"That's not good birthday behavior, Ralph," said
Sarah.

They went out to buy party favors. Ralph ran
through the store blowing horns and wearing a
birthday hat.

"Calm down," said Sarah. "This is not the time
to start your party."

On the way home Rotten Ralph saw a fire truck.

"I want that for my birthday," he thought.

He jumped on the fire truck and turned on the water.

"You can't have a fire truck," said Sarah.

Then they passed a stable.

"I've always wanted a pony," Ralph thought.

"Give that back," said Sarah.

When they got home Sarah baked Ralph a cake.

He licked off all the icing.

"You'd better behave yourself, Ralph," Sarah said,

"or you can't have a birthday party."

Ralph broke open the piñata and ate all the candy.

"Rotten cats don't get birthday parties," warned Sarah.

After Sarah decorated the house, Ralph swung
on the streamers and popped the balloons.
"I've had enough of your rotten behavior,"
said Sarah. "No birthday party for you!"

"I don't want a party anyway," Ralph thought.

"I just want my present."

"Go to your room," ordered Sarah. "And don't come down until you have learned how to behave."

Ralph searched through the trunks in the attic.

But he couldn't find his present.

"She must have taken it back to the store,"

he thought.

On the way back to his room he saw that Sarah

had turned off the lights.

"I guess she really means no party," Ralph

thought.

He sadly started down the stairs.

Suddenly the lights came on.

"SURPRISE!" shouted Sarah.

"SURPRISE!" shouted his friends.

"Oh Ralph, you know I love you too much
to skip your birthday," said Sarah.

Everyone had a great time. First they played pin the tail on the donkey. Then they played musical chairs. And afterward they danced.

Then Sarah gave Ralph his present.

"Happy birthday," she sang.

Rotten Ralph ripped it open.

It was a set of paints.

"I love this present," Ralph said to himself.

"Happy birthday to me."